O'CLOCK

Illustrated by Mary McQuillan

It's 4 o'cluck in the morning.
Another day is dawning...

Colin the rooster
puffs out his chest.
Ready to do
what he doodle doos best.

5 o'cluck. The farmer appears.
With toast in his hand and soap round his ears.

5.05. He unlocks the door.
Rattles his bucket. Throws corn on the floor.

We gobble our breakfast in ten seconds flat.
Jessie's the fastest (that's why she's so fat).

6 until 8. We sit on our nests. We lay white eggs or brown eggs.

(Marge does requests.)

Just after 8 we leave the hen coop.
And stroll round the farmyard all in one group.

From 9 until 10 we go our own ways.
The dust bath is Freda's,
the hopscotch
is Faye's.

11 o'cluck. We meet by the plough.
Squabble and squawk about what to do now.

If the tractor's been busy, we might hunt for worms.
Big ones, little ones, anything that squirms.

12 o'cluck. We sit in the trees.
Ambush some caterpillars, lacewings and bees.

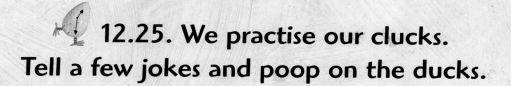 **12.25. We practise our clucks.**
Tell a few jokes and poop on the ducks.

1.02. We walk down the lane.

Jane is the blackbird who lives in the hedge.

Jane is an expert on earwigs and slugs.

One for the exercise. Two to see Jane.

She has a family of four and a husband called Reg.

She knows where to find the tastiest bugs.

 2 o'cluck. We play hide-and-seek.
Valerie should learn to tuck in her beak.

 3 o'cluck. We lie on our backs.

We make shapes in the clouds and then we make tracks.

4 o'cluck. We're back in the yard.
Wally the Collie is standing on guard.

Call him a guard dog? He's totally useless.
Woofless, furless and totally toothless.

4.15. We go
to the stable.

To visit the horses,
Molly and Mabel.

4.30 till 5. We perch in the rafters.
Watch them eat tea and hope for some afters.

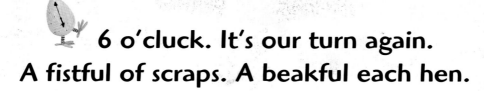 6 o'cluck. It's our turn again.
A fistful of scraps. A beakful each hen.

7 o'cluck. We form a long line.
And wait for the farmer to give us the sign.

When he jangles the keys from inside his pocket,
points to the hen house and bangs on his bucket...

We race to the coop in fifty-eighth gear.
(Last one in gets a toe up the rear.)

Last to their perch is a big rotten egg!
(Anne isn't playing. She's got a bad leg.)

The farmer locks up and goes in for tea.
It smells like pork chops and gravy to me.

7.30. We're ready for bed. No one is tired, so we natter instead.

 8 o'cluck. The sun starts to fade.

The hen house grows darker. Light turns to shade.

9 o'cluck. The farmer shows up.
With hot milky coffee in his favourite blue cup.

He rattles our door and checks all the locks.
We sit on our perch and wait for the fox.

The fox is called Olga. She lives in the woods.
She eats chickens for supper. She'd eat us if she could.

Brenda starts fidgeting at twenty to ten.
Any time now will be fox-time again.

At 10.57 we all hear a sound.

Something is sniffing

and snuffling around.

The noises are coming from
the farmhouse back door.

Bin bags are spilling out on to the floor.

Tin cans are clanking.
Pork bones are cracking.
Sharp teeth are crunching.
Olga is snacking.

The farmer is sleeping.
He doesn't hear her.
But we can hear sounds creeping nearer and nearer.

Metres or centimetres, it's too dark to tell.
But Olga is close.
We can tell by the smell.

Colin stays calm
and jumps to the floor.
Just to the left of the
crack in the door.

Through the hole in the wood, he wiggles a feather.
(Very kindly donated by Heather.)

He wiggles it, jiggles it and now you'll see why.

It's greedy, it's beady, it's nasty and vulgar.
It's stary and scary.
It's definitely Olga.

Before Olga can blink, Colin scoops up some dirt.
And cops her an eyeful, right where it hurts.

Olga runs off with a flea in each ear.
That will teach her to come sniffing round here.

It's 12 o'cluck midnight. Everyone's yawning.
Time for some sleep. Only four hours till morning!

THE HEND